DATE DUE

A NOTE TO PARENTS

When your children are ready to "step into reading," giving them the right books is as crucial to their development as giving them the right food to eat. **Step into Reading®** books and **Star Wars®** **Jedi Readers** feature exciting stories and information reinforced with lively, colorful illustrations that make learning to read fun, satisfying, and rewarding. We have even taken *extra* steps to keep your child engaged by offering Step into Reading Sticker books, Step into Reading Math books, and Step into Reading Phonics books, in addition to fabulous fiction and nonfiction.

Learning to read, Step by Step:

- **Super Early** books (Preschool–Kindergarten) support pre-reading skills. Parent and child can engage in "see and say" reading using the strong picture cues and the few simple words on each page.

- **Early** books (Preschool–Kindergarten) let emergent readers tackle one or two short sentences of large type per page.

- **Step 1** books (Preschool–Grade 1) have the same easy-to-read type as Early, but with more words per page.

- **Step 2** books (Grades 1–3) offer longer and slightly more difficult text while introducing contractions and clauses. Children are often drawn to our exciting natural science nonfiction titles at this level.

- **Step 3** books (Grades 2–3) present paragraphs, chapters, and fully developed plot lines in fiction and nonfiction.

- **Step 4** books (Grades 2–4) feature thrilling fiction and nonfiction illustrated with exciting photographs for independent as well as reluctant readers.

Remember: The grade levels assigned to the six steps are intended only as guides. Some children move through all six steps rapidly; others climb the steps over a period of a few years. Either way, these books will help children "step into reading" for life!

To Alice Alfonsi, whose tremendous efforts have made this
adventure possible
—M.C.

Dedicated to my son Henry, who made Star Wars *new again*
—T.L.E.

Library of Congress Cataloging-in-Publication Data
Cerasini, Marc A., 1952–
Star Wars. Anakin: Apprentice / by Marc Cerasini ; illustrated by Tommy Lee
Edwards. p. cm. — (Jedi readers. A step 4 book) SUMMARY: Nineteen-year-old
Anakin Skywalker, apprentice to Obi-Wan Kenobi, remembers some of his past
adventures in which he raced swoop bikes, built androids, and found crystals to
complete his lightsaber. ISBN 0-375-81463-9 (trade) — ISBN 0-375-91463-3 (lib. bdg.)
[1. Science fiction.] I. Edwards, Tommy Lee, ill. II. Title. III. Jedi readers.
Step 4 book. PZ7.C3185 Sr 2002 [Fic]—dc21 2001048984

www.randomhouse.com/kids

Official *Star Wars* Web sites:
www.starwars.com
www.starwarskids.com

Printed in the United States of America First Edition April 2002 10 9 8 7 6 5 4 3 2 1

STEP INTO READING, RANDOM HOUSE, and the Random House colophon are registered
trademarks of Random House, Inc.

JEDI READERS

STAR WARS®

ANAKIN: APPRENTICE

BY MARC CERASINI

ILLUSTRATED BY TOMMY LEE EDWARDS

A Step 4 Book

Random House
New York

LUCAS BOOKS

1
A New Mission

Anakin Skywalker connected the last two wires. He snapped the control panel back into place. Then he flipped the switch.

The droid staggered to its feet, eyes flashing. Anakin smiled. Then came a shrill beep. The panel suddenly sprang open and the motivator popped out!

The droid's eyes went dark and it toppled over.

"Shouldn't you be meditating?"

Anakin looked up. His Master, Obi-Wan Kenobi, stood in the doorway.

"I tried to meditate, but I couldn't," Anakin said.

"Meditation does not come easily," Obi-Wan replied. "It takes practice."

Anakin sighed. "Life just seems so much simpler when I'm fixing things."

Obi-Wan glanced at the motionless droid. "So that droid is *fixed*?"

"Well, not yet," Anakin said sheepishly. They both laughed.

"You really should take time to meditate and focus your energy," Obi-Wan said, serious now. "We have a mission."

Anakin brightened. "A mission?"

"Do you remember Queen Amidala of Naboo?"

"Padmé!" the young Padawan said, excited now. "She's on Coruscant?"

"She's a Senator now. She has just arrived," Obi-Wan replied.

He placed his hand on Anakin's shoulder.

"Gather your equipment and prepare yourself," he said. "I'll be back for you in an hour. Senator Amidala is in danger. She needs our help."

"I'll be ready," Anakin promised.

Obi-Wan smiled. "I know," he said.

The Jedi Knight departed and Anakin began to collect his things. He would need his lightsaber and utility belt, his comlink and . . .

Anakin tried to concentrate on his list, but he couldn't stop thinking about Padmé.

He bumped into his desk, and his journal, where he kept his droid designs, fell to the floor. When Anakin stooped to pick it up, he saw a drawing of Padmé he'd made many years before.

I wonder if you've changed over these past ten years, Anakin thought. *I know I have.*

2
Remembering

Ten years earlier, Anakin had left his mother and come to the Jedi Temple. Life as a Padawan learner was much better than life as a slave. However, Anakin quickly discovered that becoming a Jedi would not be easy. There were always lessons to learn and challenges to face. There was so much work, and so little time for fun!

Obi-Wan was very strict. He made Anakin work hard at everything, but he was loving and fair, too.

Anakin tried to do his best, but he sometimes failed. When he did, Obi-Wan was there to scold him and to teach him. Sometimes it seemed his Master didn't notice the good things, only his mistakes. Still, Anakin loved Obi-Wan like a father.

Anakin enjoyed building things. Back home on Tatooine he had built C-3PO, so Anakin built another droid for his new home in the Jedi Temple.

LE-4DO wasn't very smart, but he was useful. The little droid helped Anakin with his chores.

Anakin decided to build more helpers to perform the tasks he hated to do. Soon his droids were all over the place!

They swept the halls of the Jedi Temple. They tended plants in the gardens. They cleaned his room and folded his clothes.

Master Obi-Wan was uneasy about all these droids. "When I was a Padawan, I did my own chores," he said.

But Anakin didn't listen. He was proud. His droids did all the dirty work, so there was more time for him to study and become a Jedi.

3
Droid on the Rampage

Not all of Anakin's droids operated properly. Sometimes they broke down. Sometimes they went a little crazy.

When Anakin was twelve, he built a fighting droid to help him practice. One day he brought it to a training session taught by Mace Windu.

"What's this?" Mace asked.

"A fighting droid," Anakin said proudly. "I built it to help us better our skills."

"Wait, Anakin. I don't think you should—"

Before Mace could finish, Anakin powered up the droid.

Suddenly there was a loud pop. The fighting droid's mechanical brain blew up.

"*Bzzzzt* . . . Swing. Block. Reverse. Strike . . . *Bzzzzt!*"

The droid's arms popped out. Its laser
eyes opened fire!

Energy bolts shot everywhere.

The Padawans scattered!

Master Windu tackled the droid and switched it off. The droid crashed to the floor.

Mace frowned at Anakin. "Well, that *was* quite a lesson, young Padawan," he said. "But not the lesson I had in mind."

Later, Obi-Wan caught up with Anakin. "Meditating about the error of your ways?" teased Obi-Wan.

"I didn't mean to wreck the training session," Anakin cried. "I was just trying to help! To make things easier."

Obi-Wan sat down next to his apprentice. "Not everything that makes life easy is good for us. If droids did everything for us, we would soon lose our skills."

"They could just do the hard stuff," Anakin replied. "The stuff we don't want to do."

Obi-Wan shook his head. "It's doing the hard things, facing the challenges, that helps us grow."

Anakin nodded. Perhaps Obi-Wan was right.

4
The Garbage Pits

I need to find a challenge, Anakin decided. *I need to try something new and difficult.*

Life at the Jedi Temple was hard, but it no longer seemed a *challenge.* Anakin's connection to the Force was too strong.

One night, while he watched the lights of Coruscant far below, Anakin wondered if he could find a new challenge down there. He decided to sneak out of the Jedi Temple and find out.

Anakin had traveled the city before, but always with Obi-Wan. He had never gone out alone, and never at night.

As he wandered the streets, Anakin saw amazing things. Strange creatures who came from all over the galaxy. Gigantic buildings glittering with light. Thousands of speeders racing across the sky.

Then Anakin saw a strange device on the back of a speeder.

"What's that?" he asked.

"Racing wings," the owner replied. "I'm going to the Wicko District. There are races at the garbage pits."

Anakin decided to go, too.

The races were amazing! The racers flew over the garbage pits of Coruscant. Giant worms lurked at the bottom, squirming in a sea of liquid silicon.

Every few minutes, garbage canisters were blasted into space. Unlucky racers got blasted into space, too.

Wow! These wings are just as dangerous as the Podracers I used to fly. I have to try them!

Anakin couldn't wait to face this new challenge. He got his own harness and wings, then entered a race.

He ran into trouble at the starting line. As he waited for the competition to begin, Anakin stood near a nasty alien called a Blood Carver.

The creature sneered at him. "You smell like a slave."

Suddenly the Blood Carver attacked. Anakin jumped into the pit to escape. The savage alien jumped in after him.

The Blood Carver slashed the wing of Anakin's glider. Anakin plunged to the bottom of the pit.

He looked up and saw the Blood Carver charging at him.

Suddenly Obi-Wan swooped out of the sky.

His lightsaber crackled. The Blood Carver howled. Obi-Wan had cut the wings off the creature's racing harness!

Then the Jedi dived down and grabbed Anakin.

"Obi-Wan! Thanks for the rescue," Anakin cried.

Together they blasted out of the pit. When they were safe, Obi-Wan threw the racing wings into the pit and turned to his apprentice.

"What were you thinking?" Obi-Wan said. "Don't you know those races are dangerous?"

"It's a *challenge*," Anakin replied. "You told me challenge was good."

Obi-Wan thought for a moment, then smiled.

"You're right, I did," he said. "At least you're listening. I only wish you would *understand*."

"Understand what?" Anakin said, puzzled.

Obi-Wan sighed. "That looking for excitement and adventure is not the Jedi way."

5
Anakin's Quest

Months later, Anakin and his Master went on a dangerous journey to the frozen planet Ilum.

Anakin piloted the sleek transport himself. Obi-Wan guided him to a ledge on a gleaming ice mountain and told him to land.

"Why are we here?" Anakin asked his Master.

"We are here not on a mission, but a quest," Obi-Wan replied. "We will go to the Crystal Cave, where you will gather the crystals to complete your lightsaber."

Outside, the air was frigid. The wind blew and the ice was slippery. The climb to the cave was long and dangerous.

"Why keep the crystals here?" Anakin cried over the howl of the wind. "It's so hard to reach them."

"The crystals grow in this cave,"
Obi-Wan replied. "The challenge is part of
the reward."

They both smiled, recalling the last time
Obi-Wan had spoken to Anakin about
challenge.

Near the top of the icy peak they found the Crystal Cave. But the Jedi were not alone. The entrance was guarded by a pack of fierce, hulking predators.

"Gorgodons," Obi-Wan said. "They have triple rows of teeth and sharp claws. If they catch you, they'll squeeze you to death."

The biggest gorgodon saw them and lurched forward.

"Anything else I should know?" Anakin asked.

"Gorgodons can only be stopped by a blow to the back of the neck—"

With a roar the creature charged.

"And watch out for their—"

A reptilian tail lashed out, slapping Anakin and sending him flying.

"—tails!" Obi-Wan shouted, activating his lightsaber.

The Jedi Knight slashed at the creature, but the gorgodon grabbed him and began to squeeze. Obi-Wan was helpless.

Suddenly the gorgodon howled and released him. The creature staggered and dropped at Obi-Wan's feet. Anakin had used the cable launcher to slay the creature!

The rest of the gorgodons fled. Obi-Wan led Anakin to the entrance of the Crystal Cave.

"The crystals are deep within," Obi-Wan explained. "There will be visions and voices. Some may frighten you."

"What are they?" Anakin asked.

"They are your deepest fears," Obi-Wan said. "That is what you must face."

Anakin removed his cold-weather gear. He stood in the freezing wind wearing his Jedi robes.

"I am ready," Anakin said.

Obi-Wan handed Anakin a pouch. "Here is the hilt you constructed. You will finish the lightsaber with your own hands."

Anakin heard a ghostly whisper. The sound made him shiver.

"You must go forward alone," Obi-Wan
said. "Remember, there are lessons to be
learned from fear and anger."

"I know," Anakin replied.

"No, you do not," Obi-Wan said. "But you
will."

6
The Vision

Inside the cave, the walls were covered with strange markings—the history of the Jedi, carved in stone.

Anakin saw an eerie glow on the floor of the cave. The crystals!

Anakin chose three crystals that seemed to speak to him.

"Before you begin you must meditate."

The voice startled Anakin. He turned and saw Obi-Wan. Wasn't Anakin supposed to be alone?

Suddenly Obi-Wan's face changed. His skin became scarlet. Horns sprouted from his bald head. His eyes turned yellow and savage. Anakin saw blackness and evil.

It was the Sith that had killed Qui-Gon!

The monster laughed, then tossed something to Anakin. He snatched it out of the air.

It was Anakin's lightsaber. It was complete! The hilt was perfectly crafted and beautifully balanced.

Anakin activated the blade and attacked Qui-Gon's murderer.

"I am the Master you secretly want," the evil one hissed as he dodged Anakin's blow.

"No!" Anakin screamed. "You're a vision. I can make you go away."

"I am the dark side, and I am part of you," the Sith replied. Then the creature activated a double-bladed lightsaber. He smiled, his razor-sharp teeth gleaming in the darkness.

Anakin charged. The fiend snarled and knocked him aside.

Anakin was dashed against the wall of the cave. He slumped to the floor. Dazed, he heard the Sith laugh.

"I will return," he said. "For I dwell inside you."

When Anakin opened his eyes again, the lightsaber was by his side.

I must have completed it in the trance, he told himself.

When Anakin emerged from the Crystal Cave, Obi-Wan was waiting for him.

"Look what you have done," Obi-Wan said proudly. "This lightsaber is magnificent. The Force is truly with you."

Anakin didn't tell Obi-Wan about his troubling vision. He was happy to have his own lightsaber. He finally felt like a Jedi, so he focused on that.

Still, he remained troubled by the creature's words.

Can such evil really live inside me? Anakin wondered.

7
A Double Life

After they returned from Ilum, Anakin and Obi-Wan went on many missions together and had many adventures. Anakin's connection to the Force continued to grow. So did his restless nature.

Once again, Anakin searched for challenge and excitement. He became fascinated by Coruscant's underworld. At night he prowled the twisting avenues of the lower levels.

One night Anakin saw a crowd of teenagers gathering around the entrance to a cargo tunnel.

"What's going on?" he asked.

"The leader of the Sligo Pirate gang is going to race the Twi'lek!" a teenager with purple hair said excitedly.

A race! Anakin rushed to the front of the crowd.

Two swoop bikes hovered near the tunnel's mouth, engines roaring. A rough-looking Gotal gave the signal, and the racers were off.

They roared into the tunnel and out of sight.

"What happens now?" Anakin asked.

"The winner will come out of the tunnel in a few minutes," the purple-haired girl replied.

"And the loser?"

The girl shrugged.

Suddenly there was an explosion. Seconds later, the Twi'lek sped out of the cargo shaft to cheers from the crowd.

The Sligo Pirates' leader limped out of the tunnel a moment later. There was no sign of his swoop bike.

The rest of the Sligo Pirates climbed aboard their swoop bikes. They flew away, leaving their former chief in the dust.

"Looks like they'll have to choose a new leader," said Purple Hair.

As dawn broke, Anakin walked back to the Jedi Temple. He was burning with excitement.

Oollie, the girl with the purple hair, had explained how the races worked. The contestants came from all over Coruscant. They raced through the cargo tunnels at night, when hover-train traffic was light. The competitions were very dangerous. Bikers had to dodge cargo caravans and droid maintenance teams. Sometimes they crashed.

It didn't take long for Anakin to get his own swoop bike. He loved his sleek red racer. Anakin worked on it until it was the fastest swoop around.

Almost every night he flew down to the industrial sector to race. Anakin won more than he lost.

Soon everyone who dwelled in the underworld had heard of the Jedi who raced swoop bikes. Gangs came from all over the planet to watch Anakin.

Sometimes they challenged the young
Jedi to a race.

"Someone's looking for you," Oollie told Anakin one night.

"Oh," Anakin replied, climbing off his swoop. "Who would that be?"

"Drako, the leader of the Hawk-bat gang."

Anakin was impressed. Drako was a four-armed Codru-Ji and one of the fastest racers on the planet. Drako never lost. Some said it was because he always cheated.

"Here he comes now!" Oollie said.

With a rumble that shook the buildings around them, the Hawk-bat gang raced into the square. The leader roared to a stop in front of Anakin.

"Are you the Jedi?" the gang leader asked.

"That's me."

"I challenge you to a race through the tunnel near the power plant. Meet me in one hour."

Anakin smiled. "You're on."

Drako grinned evilly. "Don't be late, Jedi."

As the gang sped away, Anakin felt a tingle. The Force was warning him of danger. Anakin stubbornly ignored his feelings.

If it wasn't dangerous, then it wouldn't be a challenge, he told himself.

8
The Deadly Race

Anakin arrived at the cargo tunnel at the appointed time. News of the race had spread quickly. There was a large crowd waiting near the power plant for the race to begin.

The Gotal who usually refereed these events was nowhere to be seen. One of the Hawk-bat gang members stood at the entrance, waving a starting flag.

Once again, Anakin sensed danger, but it was too late to back out now.

Anakin guided his swoop bike to the starting line and stopped beside Drako. The gang leader gunned his engine. His swoop bike rumbled with power.

The referee waved his flag.

"Ready . . . steady . . . BURN IT!"

The swoops took off in a cloud of dust.

Anakin was already in the lead as they sped into the cargo tunnel.

Drako was right behind him.

Inside the tunnel, Drako pulled even with Anakin. Side by side they raced, around corners and past catwalks crowded with droid maintenance teams.

Then Anakin saw Drako holding something—an ion blaster!

Drako aimed at Anakin's bike and fired. A burst of blue lightning rippled around Anakin's swoop. The engine coughed as Anakin fought for control.

Suddenly Drako swerved, darting into a narrow side tunnel and vanishing from sight.

At that moment a giant cargo carrier roared around the corner. The droid-controlled hauler filled the tunnel. There was no getting around it!

The ion bolt had damaged Anakin's engine and steering mechanism. His swoop was out of control.

Anakin leaped clear just before the cargo carrier slammed into his bike. He somersaulted in the air and landed on a catwalk.

Anakin was battered and bruised from the fall, but his Jedi training had saved his life.

9
A New Challenge

A hand settled on Anakin's shoulder, startling him.

"Anakin," Obi-Wan said. "It's time for us to meet Senator Amidala."

Anakin was surprised. Was the hour up already? He had been so lost in the events of the past that he had not noticed.

He closed the journal and grabbed his equipment.

"I'm ready," Anakin said, hurrying to the door.

"Not quite," Obi-Wan replied. He placed Anakin's lightsaber in the Padawan's hand.

"Try not to forget it next time," Obi-Wan said.

"Sorry, Master," Anakin said.

"I've told you before, a Jedi's lightsaber is his most precious possession."

"Yes, Master."

"This weapon is your life."

"You're right, Master," Anakin said impatiently. "You *have* told me before and I have heard you."

"You've heard me, but do you remember what I said?" Master Obi-Wan replied.

Anakin sighed. "I will remember from now on."

"Perhaps," Obi-Wan said with an eyebrow raised.

Then the Jedi Knight pushed his Padawan to the door.

"Come, Anakin," he said. "The Senator awaits."

Obi-Wan and Anakin flew through the crowded skies of Coruscant, toward Senator Amidala's apartments.

Anakin tingled with excitement. He couldn't wait to see Padmé again.

"The situation is grave," Obi-Wan informed his apprentice. "Assassins tried to murder Senator Amidala."

"Who would dare?" Anakin demanded.

"We don't know."

"What exactly is our mission?"

"The Jedi Council wants us to protect the Senator," Obi-Wan said.

Anakin nodded. "Then we must find out who is trying to hurt Padmé—I mean, Senator Amidala. We must hunt them down and stop them."

"No, you misunderstand the mission," Obi-Wan corrected. "We are here to *protect* the Senator, not start our own investigation."

"We're only supposed to protect her? Where's the challenge in that?" Anakin exclaimed as they entered the lobby of the apartment building.

"This is not a time to create a challenge for yourself. It is a time to obey your elders."

"We'll see," Anakin whispered as the doors closed and the turbolift began to rise.